中国红 CHINESE RED　传 承 笔 记

个人信息

U0062930

个人信息
PERSONAL INFOMATION

中 国 茶

Chinese Tea

中国是茶的故乡。中国人最早发现、栽培和饮用茶叶,并将茶叶种子、采制技术、品茶技艺等传播到全世界。茶兴于中国的唐代,在丝绸、瓷器向国外输出的同时,茶叶也逐渐传播至国外,并越来越受到国外人的青睐。

中国茶种类繁多、名茶荟萃。在中国广大的产茶区域内,但凡有名山的地方,几乎都产有名茶,如武林山龙井茶、顾渚山紫笋茶、普陀山佛茶、洞庭山碧螺春、黄山毛峰茶、庐山云雾茶、峨眉山竹叶青茶、蒙山蒙顶茶、君山银针茶、六大茶山普洱茶、太姥山绿雪芽茶、武夷山大红袍茶、凤凰山单丛茶、冻顶山乌龙茶等。这些茶各具特色,共同代表了中国茶的品质。

在中国古代,人们也将饮茶与品行修养联系在一起,讲求品茶悟道的文化情韵。对于中国人来说,茶虽然不是饭,不能果腹,却非喝不可。饮茶是中国人奉行的生活文化。每当有客人来访,主人就会沏上一壶茶来招待客人,这种习俗一直延续到现在。在宴请客人时,主人有时会用酒来表达敬意,而茶是唯一能代替酒的饮品,"以茶代酒"既不失礼仪,又令人愉快。茶不仅是中国人日常和宴客的饮品,也是婚礼、生日或葬礼等大型聚会时不可或缺的饮品。

时至今日,随着人们对健康的重视,中国茶更以其独特的保健功效再一次掀起了饮茶热潮。

中国茶

Chinese Tea

China is the hometown of tea. Chinese people were the first to discover, cultivate, and drink tea. They spread tea seed, tea picking and processing techniques, and tea appreciation techniques to the rest of the world. Tea began to gain fame in the Tang Dynasty (618–907) and was gradually exported to other countries together with other specialties of China such as silk and chinaware. It was loved by more and more people in the world.

There is a large variety of tea in China and many of them are famous ones. China has vast tea-producing areas. Almost all the great mountains in the country produce famous teas, such as Longjing (Dragon Well) Tea from Mt. Wulin, Zisun (Purple Bamboo Shoot) Tea from Mt. Guzhu, Buddha Tea from Mt. Putuo, Biluochun (Green Spiral Spring) Tea from Mt. Dongting, Maofeng (Hairy Tip) Tea from Mt. Huangshan, Yunwu (Cloud and Mist) Tea from Mt. Lushan, Zhuyeqing (Green Bamboo Leaf) Tea from Mt. Emei, Mengding (Mt. Mengshan Summit) Tea from Mt. Mengshan, Yinzhen (Silver Tip) Tea from Mt. Junshan, Pu'er Tea from Six Major Tea Mountains, Luxueya (Green Snow Bud) Tea from Mt. Taimu, Dahongpao (Big Red Robe) Tea from Mt. Wuyi, Dancong (Single Clump) Tea from Mt. Phoenix, Oolong Tea from Mt. Dongding, etc. These teas have different characteristics and represent the common quality of Chinese tea.

In ancient China, people associated tea drinking with character building and laid stress on the cultural charm in tea appreciation and philosophical realization. For the Chinese, although tea does not fill their stomach like rice, they just cannot do without it. Drinking tea is a life culture upheld by Chinese people. When guests come, the host will always make a cup of tea to treat them. This custom has been passed down to this day. When entertaining guests with a banquet, the host will sometimes propose a toast to the guests to show his respect. Tea is the only qualified substitute for the wine on this occasion. It meets the protocol and keeps everybody happy. Tea is an indispensable drink for Chinese people in their daily life and during formal gatherings such as wedding, birthday party, or funeral.

Today, with people paying greater attention to health, Chinese tea is again popular due to its unique health-care efficacy.

2014 年

一月 / January

日	一	二	三	四	五	六
			1 元旦节	2 初二	3 初三	4 初四
5 小寒	6 初六	7 初七	8 初八	9 初九	10 初十	11 十一
12 十二	13 十三	14 十四	15 十五	16 十六	17 十七	18 十八
19 十九	20 大寒	21 廿一	22 廿二	23 廿三	24 廿四	25 廿五
26 廿六	27 廿七	28 廿八	29 廿九	30 除夕	31 春节	

二月 / February

日	一	二	三	四	五	六
						1 初二
2 初三	3 初四	4 立春	5 初六	6 初七	7 初八	8 初九
9 初十	10 十一	11 十二	12 十三	13 十四	14 元宵节	15 十六
16 十七	17 十八	18 十九	19 雨水	20 廿一	21 廿二	22 廿三
23 廿四	24 廿五	25 廿六	26 廿七	27 廿八	28 廿九	

三月 / March

日	一	二	三	四	五	六
						1 二月
2 初二	3 初三	4 初四	5 初五	6 惊蛰	7 初七	8 妇女节
9 初九	10 初十	11 十一	12 植树节	13 十三	14 十四	15 十五
16 十六	17 十七	18 十八	19 十九	20 廿一	21 春分	22 廿三
23 廿四	24 廿五	25 廿六	26 廿七	27 廿八	28 廿九	29 廿九
30 三十	31 三月					

四月 / April

日	一	二	三	四	五	六
		1 愚人节	2 初三	3 初四	4 初五	5 清明节
6 初七	7 初八	8 初九	9 初十	10 十一	11 十二	12 十三
13 十四	14 十五	15 十六	16 十七	17 十八	18 十九	19 二十
20 谷雨	21 廿二	22 廿三	23 廿四	24 廿五	25 廿六	26 廿七
27 廿八	28 廿九	29 四月	30 初二			

五月 / May

日	一	二	三	四	五	六
				1 劳动节	2 初四	3 初五
4 青年节	5 立夏	6 初八	7 初九	8 初十	9 十一	10 十二
11 母亲节	12 十四	13 十五	14 十六	15 十七	16 十八	17 十九
18 二十	19 廿一	20 廿二	21 小满	22 廿四	23 廿五	24 廿六
25 廿七	26 廿八	27 廿九	28 三十	29 五月	30 初二	31 初三

六月 / June

日	一	二	三	四	五	六
1 儿童节	2 端午节	3 初六	4 初七	5 初八	6 芒种	7 初十
8 十一	9 十二	10 十三	11 十四	12 十五	13 十六	14 十七
15 父亲节	16 十九	17 二十	18 廿一	19 廿二	20 廿三	21 夏至
22 廿五	23 廿六	24 廿七	25 廿八	26 廿九	27 六月	28 初二
29 初三	30 初四					

七月 / July

日	一	二	三	四	五	六
		1 建党节	2 初六	3 初七	4 初八	5 初九
6 初十	7 小暑	8 十二	9 十三	10 十四	11 十五	12 十六
13 十七	14 十八	15 十九	16 二十	17 廿一	18 廿二	19 廿三
20 廿四	21 廿五	22 廿六	23 大暑	24 廿八	25 廿九	26 三十
27 七月	28 初二	29 初三	30 初四	31 初五		

八月 / August

日	一	二	三	四	五	六
					1 建军节	2 初七
3 初八	4 初九	5 初十	6 十一	7 立秋	8 十三	9 十四
10 十五	11 十六	12 十七	13 十八	14 十九	15 二十	16 廿一
17 廿二	18 廿三	19 廿四	20 廿五	21 廿六	22 廿七	23 处暑
24 廿九	25 三十	26 八月	27 初二	28 初三	29 初四	30 初五
31 初七						

九月 / September

日	一	二	三	四	五	六
	1 初八	2 初九	3 初十	4 十一	5 十二	6 十三
7 十四	8 白露/中秋节	9 十六	10 教师节	11 十八	12 十九	13 二十
14 廿一	15 廿二	16 廿三	17 廿四	18 廿五	19 廿六	20 廿七
21 廿八	22 廿九	23 秋分	24 九月	25 初二	26 初三	27 初四
28 初五	29 初六	30 初七				

十月 / October

日	一	二	三	四	五	六
			1 国庆节	2 重阳节	3 初十	4 十一
5 十二	6 十三	7 十四	8 寒露	9 十六	10 十七	11 十八
12 十九	13 二十	14 廿一	15 廿二	16 廿三	17 十四	18 廿五
19 廿六	20 廿七	21 廿八	22 廿九	23 霜降	24 闰九月	25 初二
26 初三	27 初四	28 初五	29 初六	30 初七	31 初八	

十一月 / November

日	一	二	三	四	五	六
						1 初九
2 初十	3 十一	4 十二	5 十三	6 十四	7 立冬	8 十六
9 十七	10 十八	11 十九	12 二十	13 廿一	14 廿二	15 廿三
16 廿四	17 廿五	18 廿六	19 廿七	20 廿八	21 廿九	22 小雪
23 初二	24 初三	25 初四	26 初五	27 初六	28 初七	29 初八
30 初九						

十二月 / December

日	一	二	三	四	五	六
	1 初十	2 十一	3 十二	4 十三	5 十四	6 十五
7 大雪	8 十七	9 十八	10 十九	11 二十	12 廿一	13 廿二
14 廿三	15 廿四	16 廿五	17 廿六	18 廿七	19 廿八	20 廿九
21 廿一	22 冬至	23 初二	24 初三	25 圣诞节	26 初五	27 初六
28 初七	29 初八	30 初九	31 初十			

2015 年

一月 / January

日	一	二	三	四	五	六
				1 元旦节	2 十二	3 十三
4 十四	5 十五	6 小寒	7 十七	8 十八	9 十九	10 二十
11 廿一	12 廿二	13 廿三	14 廿四	15 廿五	16 廿六	17 廿七
18 廿八	19 廿九	20 大寒	21 腊月	22 初二	23 初三	24 初四
25 初六	26 初七	27 初八	28 初九	29 初十	30 十一	31 十二

二月 / February

日	一	二	三	四	五	六
1 十三	2 十四	3 十五	4 立春	5 十七	6 十八	7 十九
8 二十	9 廿一	10 廿二	11 廿三	12 廿四	13 廿五	14 廿六
15 廿七	16 廿八	17 廿九	18 除夕	19 春节/雨水	20 初二	21 初三
22 初四	23 初五	24 初六	25 初七	26 初八	27 初九	28 初十

三月 / March

日	一	二	三	四	五	六
1 十一	2 十二	3 十三	4 十四	5 元宵节	6 惊蛰	7 十七
8 妇女节	9 十九	10 二十	11 廿一	12 植树节	13 廿三	14 廿四
15 廿五	16 廿六	17 廿七	18 廿八	19 廿九	20 二月	21 春分
22 初三	23 初四	24 初五	25 初六	26 初七	27 初八	28 初九
29 初十	30 十一	31 十二				

四月 / April

日	一	二	三	四	五	六
			1 愚人节	2 十四	3 十五	4 十六
5 清明节	6 十八	7 十九	8 二十	9 廿一	10 廿二	11 廿三
12 廿四	13 廿五	14 廿六	15 廿七	16 廿八	17 廿九	18 三十
19 三月	20 谷雨	21 初三	22 初四	23 初五	24 初六	25 初七
26 初八	27 初九	28 初十	29 十一	30 十二		

五月 / May

日	一	二	三	四	五	六
					1 劳动节	2 十四
3 十五	4 青年节	5 十七	6 立夏	7 十九	8 二十	9 廿一
10 母亲节	11 廿三	12 廿四	13 廿五	14 廿六	15 廿七	16 廿八
17 廿九	18 四月	19 初二	20 初三	21 小满	22 初五	23 初六
24 初七	25 初八	26 初九	27 初十	28 十一	29 十二	30 十三
31 十四						

六月 / June

日	一	二	三	四	五	六
	1 儿童节	2 十六	3 十七	4 十八	5 十九	6 芒种
7 廿一	8 廿二	9 廿三	10 廿四	11 廿五	12 廿六	13 廿七
14 廿八	15 廿九	16 五月	17 初二	18 初三	19 初四	20 端午节
21 父亲节	22 夏至	23 初八	24 初九	25 初十	26 十一	27 十二
28 十三	29 十四	30 十五				

七月 / July

日	一	二	三	四	五	六
			1 建党节	2 十七	3 十八	4 十九
5 二十	6 廿一	7 小暑	8 廿三	9 廿四	10 廿五	11 廿六
12 廿七	13 廿八	14 廿九	15 三十	16 六月	17 初二	18 初三
19 初四	20 初五	21 初六	22 初七	23 大暑	24 初九	25 初十
26 十一	27 十二	28 十三	29 十四	30 十五	31 十六	

八月 / August

日	一	二	三	四	五	六
						1 建军节
2 十八	3 十九	4 二十	5 廿一	6 廿二	7 廿三	8 立秋
9 廿五	10 廿六	11 廿七	12 廿八	13 廿九	14 七月	15 初二
16 初三	17 初四	18 初五	19 初六	20 初七	21 初八	22 初九
23 初十	24 十一	25 十二	26 十三	27 十四	28 十五	29 十六
30 十七	31 十八					

九月 / September

日	一	二	三	四	五	六
		1 十九	2 二十	3 廿一	4 廿二	5 廿三
6 廿四	7 廿五	8 白露	9 教师节	10 廿八	11 廿九	12 三十
13 八月	14 初二	15 初三	16 初四	17 初五	18 初六	19 初七
20 初八	21 初九	22 初十	23 秋分	24 十二	25 十三	26 十四
27 中秋节	28 十六	29 十七	30 十八			

十月 / October

日	一	二	三	四	五	六
				1 国庆节	2 二十	3 廿一
4 廿二	5 廿三	6 廿四	7 廿五	8 寒露	9 廿七	10 廿八
11 廿九	12 三十	13 九月	14 初二	15 初三	16 初四	17 初五
18 初六	19 初七	20 初八	21 重阳节	22 初十	23 霜降	24 十二
25 十三	26 十四	27 十五	28 十六	29 十七	30 十八	31 十九

十一月 / November

日	一	二	三	四	五	六
1 二十	2 廿一	3 廿二	4 廿三	5 廿四	6 廿五	7 廿六
8 立冬	9 廿八	10 廿九	11 十月	12 初二	13 初三	14 初四
15 初五	16 初六	17 初七	18 初八	19 初九	20 初十	21 十一
22 小雪	23 十三	24 十四	25 十五	26 十六	27 十七	28 十八
29 十九	30 二十					

十二月 / December

日	一	二	三	四	五	六
		1 二十	2 廿一	3 廿二	4 廿三	5 廿四
6 廿五	7 大雪	8 廿七	9 廿八	10 廿九	11 十一月	12 初二
13 初三	14 初四	15 初五	16 初六	17 初七	18 初八	19 初九
20 初十	21 十一	22 冬至	23 十三	24 十四	25 圣诞节	26 十六
27 十七	28 十八	29 十九	30 二十	31 廿一		

2016 年

一月 / January

日	一	二	三	四	五	六
					1 元旦节	2 廿三
3 廿四	4 廿五	5 廿六	6 小寒	7 廿八	8 廿九	9 三十
10 腊月	11 初二	12 初三	13 初四	14 初五	15 初六	16 初七
17 初八	18 初九	19 初十	20 大寒	21 十二	22 十三	23 十四
24 十五	25 十六	26 十七	27 十八	28 十九	29 二十	30 廿一
31 廿二						

二月 / February

日	一	二	三	四	五	六
	1 廿三	2 廿四	3 廿五	4 立春	5 廿七	6 廿八
7 除夕	8 春节	9 初二	10 初三	11 初四	12 初五	13 初六
14 初七	15 初八	16 初九	17 初十	18 十一	19 雨水	20 十三
21 十四	22 元宵节	23 十六	24 十七	25 十八	26 十九	27 二十
28 廿一	29 廿二					

三月 / March

日	一	二	三	四	五	六
		1 廿三	2 廿四	3 廿五	4 廿六	5 惊蛰
6 廿八	7 廿九	8 妇女节	9 二月	10 初二	11 初三	12 植树节
13 初五	14 初六	15 初七	16 初八	17 初九	18 初十	19 十一
20 春分	21 十三	22 十四	23 十五	24 十六	25 十七	26 十八
27 十九	28 二十	29 廿一	30 廿二	31 廿三		

四月 / April

日	一	二	三	四	五	六
					1 愚人节	2 廿五
3 廿六	4 清明节	5 廿八	6 廿九	7 三月	8 初二	9 初三
10 初四	11 初五	12 初六	13 初七	14 初八	15 初九	16 初十
17 十一	18 十二	19 谷雨	20 十四	21 十五	22 十六	23 十七
24 十八	25 十九	26 二十	27 廿一	28 廿二	29 廿三	30 廿四

五月 / May

日	一	二	三	四	五	六
1 劳动节	2 廿六	3 廿七	4 青年节	5 立夏	6 三十	7 四月
8 母亲节	9 初三	10 初四	11 初五	12 初六	13 初七	14 初八
15 初九	16 初十	17 十一	18 十二	19 十三	20 小满	21 十五
22 十六	23 十七	24 十八	25 十九	26 二十	27 廿一	28 廿二
29 廿三	30 廿四	31 廿五				

六月 / June

日	一	二	三	四	五	六
			1 儿童节	2 廿七	3 廿八	4 廿九
5 芒种	6 初二	7 初三	8 初四	9 端午节	10 初六	11 初七
12 初八	13 初九	14 初十	15 十一	16 十二	17 十三	18 十四
19 父亲节	20 十六	21 夏至	22 十八	23 十九	24 二十	25 廿一
26 廿二	27 廿三	28 廿四	29 廿五	30 廿六		

七月 / July

日	一	二	三	四	五	六
					1 建党节	2 廿八
3 廿九	4 六月	5 初二	6 初三	7 小暑	8 初五	9 初六
10 初七	11 初八	12 初九	13 初十	14 十一	15 十二	16 十三
17 十四	18 十五	19 十六	20 十七	21 十八	22 大暑	23 二十
24 廿一	25 廿二	26 廿三	27 廿四	28 廿五	29 廿六	30 廿七
31 廿八						

八月 / August

日	一	二	三	四	五	六
	1 建军节	2 三十	3 七月	4 初二	5 初三	6 初四
7 立秋	8 初六	9 初七	10 初八	11 初九	12 初十	13 十一
14 十二	15 十三	16 十四	17 十五	18 十六	19 十七	20 十八
21 十九	22 二十	23 廿一	24 处暑	25 廿三	26 廿四	27 廿五
28 廿六	29 廿七	30 廿八	31 廿九			

九月 / September

日	一	二	三	四	五	六
				1 八月	2 初二	3 初三
4 初四	5 初五	6 初六	7 白露	8 初八	9 初九	10 教师节
11 十一	12 十二	13 十三	14 十四	15 中秋节	16 十六	17 十七
18 十八	19 十九	20 二十	21 廿一	22 秋分	23 廿三	24 廿四
25 廿五	26 廿六	27 廿七	28 廿八	29 廿九	30 三十	

十月 / October

日	一	二	三	四	五	六
						1 国庆节
2 初二	3 初三	4 初四	5 初五	6 初六	7 初七	8 寒露
9 重阳节	10 初十	11 十一	12 十二	13 十三	14 十四	15 十五
16 十六	17 十七	18 十八	19 十九	20 二十	21 廿一	22 廿二
23 霜降	24 廿四	25 廿五	26 廿六	27 廿七	28 廿八	29 廿九
30 三十	31 十月					

十一月 / November

日	一	二	三	四	五	六
		1 初二	2 初三	3 初四	4 初五	5 初六
6 初七	7 立冬	8 初九	9 初十	10 十一	11 十二	12 十三
13 十四	14 十五	15 十六	16 十七	17 十八	18 十九	19 二十
20 廿一	21 廿二	22 小雪	23 廿四	24 廿五	25 廿六	26 廿七
27 廿八	28 廿九	29 三十	30 十一月 初二			

十二月 / December

日	一	二	三	四	五	六
				1 初三	2 初四	3 初五
4 初六	5 初七	6 大雪	7 初九	8 初十	9 十一	10 十二
11 十三	12 十四	13 十五	14 十六	15 十七	16 十八	17 十九
18 二十	19 廿一	20 廿二	21 冬至	22 廿四	23 廿五	24 廿六
25 圣诞节	26 廿八	27 廿九	28 三十	29 腊月	30 初二	31 初三

1　2　3　4

5　6　7　8

9　10　11　12

SUN	MON	TUE

重要一月
Important Plan

☐

☐

☐

☐

☐

☐

☐

☐

☐

☐

☐

☐

☐

☐

备注 NOTES

WED	THU	FRI	SAT

备注 NOTES

重要一月
Important Plan

☐

☐

☐

☐

☐

☐

☐

☐

☐

☐

☐

☐

☐

☐

SUN	MON	TUE

备注 NOTES

WED	THU	FRI	SAT

备注 NOTES

_____

_____

_____

_____

重要一月
Important Plan

□

□

□

□

□

□

□

□

□

□

□

□

□

SUN	MON	TUE

备注 NOTES

WED	THU	FRI	SAT

备注 NOTES

	SUN	MON	TUE

1　2　3　4

5　6　7　8

9　10　11　12

重要一月
Important Plan

☐

☐

☐

☐

☐

☐

☐

☐

☐

☐

☐

☐

☐

☐

备注 NOTES

WED	THU	FRI	SAT

备注 NOTES

SUN	MON	TUE

重要一月
Important Plan

☐

☐

☐

☐

☐

☐

☐

☐

☐

☐

☐

☐

☐

备注 NOTES

WED	THU	FRI	SAT

备注 NOTES

1	2	3	4
5	6	7	8
9	10	11	12

重要一月
Important Plan

☐

☐

☐

☐

☐

☐

☐

☐

☐

☐

☐

☐

☐

☐

SUN	MON	TUE

备注 NOTES

WED	THU	FRI	SAT

备注 NOTES

1	2	3	4
5	6	7	8
9	10	11	12

重要一月
Important Plan

☐

☐

☐

☐

☐

☐

☐

☐

☐

☐

☐

☐

☐

☐

SUN	MON	TUE

备注 NOTES

WED	THU	FRI	SAT

备注 NOTES

1	2	3	4
5	6	7	8
9	10	11	12

重要一月
Important Plan

☐

☐

☐

☐

☐

☐

☐

☐

☐

☐

☐

☐

☐

☐

SUN	MON	TUE

备注 NOTES

WED	THU	FRI	SAT

备注 NOTES

重要一月
Important Plan

☐

☐

☐

☐

☐

☐

☐

☐

☐

☐

☐

☐

☐

☐

SUN	MON	TUE

备注 NOTES

WED	THU	FRI	SAT

备注 NOTES

月
MONTHLY

1	2	3	4
5	6	7	8
9	10	11	12

重要一月
Important Plan

☐

☐

☐

☐

☐

☐

☐

☐

☐

☐

☐

☐

☐

SUN	MON	TUE

备注 NOTES

WED	THU	FRI	SAT

备注 NOTES

重要一月
Important Plan

☐

☐

☐

☐

☐

☐

☐

☐

☐

☐

☐

☐

☐

☐

SUN	MON	TUE

备注 NOTES

WED	THU	FRI	SAT

备注 NOTES

1	2	3	4
5	6	7	8
9	10	11	12

重要一月
Important Plan

□

□

□

□

□

□

□

□

□

□

□

□

□

□

SUN	MON	TUE

备注 NOTES

WED	THU	FRI	SAT

备注 NOTES

1	2	3	4
5	6	7	8
9	10	11	12

SUN	MON	TUE

重要一月
Important Plan

☐

☐

☐

☐

☐

☐

☐

☐

☐

☐

☐

☐

☐

☐

备注 NOTES

WED	THU	FRI	SAT

备注 NOTES

1	2	3	4
5	6	7	8
9	10	11	12

重要一月
Important Plan

☐

☐

☐

☐

☐

☐

☐

☐

☐

☐

☐

☐

☐

☐

SUN	MON	TUE

备注 NOTES

WED	THU	FRI	SAT

备注 NOTES

	1	2	3	4
5	6	7	8
9	10	11	12

重要一月
Important Plan

- □
- □
- □
- □
- □
- □
- □
- □
- □
- □
- □
- □
- □
- □

SUN	MON	TUE

备注 NOTES

WED	THU	FRI	SAT

备注 NOTES
_____

_____

_____

_____

日期 DATE   天气 WEATHER

时间设定 TIME	计划 TASK	☑ or ☒
		☐
		☐
		☐
		☐
		☐
		☐
		☐

特别提醒 NOTICE

中国是茶的发祥地。世界各国最初所饮的茶叶，以及引种的茶种、饮茶的方法、栽培的技术等都是直接或间接地从中国传播去的。

China is the birthplace of tea. All countries in the world received their first import of tea leaves, tea seeds, tea drinking methods, and tea cultivation techniques directly or indirectly from China.

日期 DATE 天气 WEATHER

时间设定 TIME	计划 TASK	☑ or ☒
		☐
		☐
		☐
		☐
		☐
		☐
		☐

特别提醒 NOTICE

1961年，中国考古学家在云南省发现了一棵高达32.12米的野生大茶树，树龄约达1700年，其树高和树龄在山茶属植物中均属世界第一，是目前已发现最大、最古老的野生大茶树。

In 1961, Chinese archeologists discovered in Yunnan Province a wild big tea tree which was 32.12 meters tall and about 1,700 years old. Its height and age were both world No.1 among camellia plants. It still remains the largest and oldest wild tea tree that has been found in the world.

日期 DATE　　　　　天气 WEATHER

时间设定 TIME	计划 TASK	☑ or ☒
		☐
		☐
		☐
		☐
		☐
		☐
		☐

特别提醒 NOTICE

中国史籍上有"茶兴于唐"的说法，唐代被认为是茶的黄金时代。

According to Chinese historical records, tea began to gain fame in the Tang Dynasty (618–907). The Tang Dynasty is regarded as the golden era for tea.

时间设定 TIME	计划 TASK	☑ or ☒
		☐
		☐
		☐
		☐
		☐
		☐
		☐

特别提醒 NOTICE

唐代茶分为粗茶、散茶、末茶、饼茶，以饼茶为主。

In the Tang Dynasty (618—907), tea was divided into raw tea, loose tea, dust tea, and caky tea. Among them, caky tea was the main type.

日期 DATE　　　　　　　天气 WEATHER

时间设定 TIME	计划 TASK	☑ or ☒
		☐
		☐
		☐
		☐
		☐
		☐
		☐

特别提醒 NOTICE

唐人以煮茶为主，即先将饼茶烤干，以蒸发其中的水分，干后装袋，以保持茶香，待饼茶冷却后，将其碾成细末待煮。

People in the Tang Dynasty made tea by cooking it. First, they dried the caky tea by baking. Then, they bagged the tea to keep its aroma. Later, after the tea had cooled, they ground it into fine powder for cooking.

日期 DATE　　　　　　　　天气 WEATHER

时间设定 TIME	计划 TASK	☑ or ☒
		☐
		☐
		☐
		☐
		☐
		☐
		☐

特别提醒 NOTICE

世界上第一部茶叶著作是《茶经》，为中国茶道的奠基人陆羽所著。

The Classic of Tea is the first book on tea in the world. It was written by Lu Yu, founder of Chinese tea ceremony.

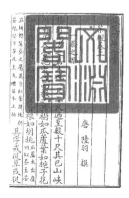

日期 DATE　　　　　　　　　天气 WEATHER

时间设定 TIME	计划 TASK	☑ or ☒
		☐
		☐
		☐
		☐
		☐
		☐
		☐

特别提醒 NOTICE

西湖龙井茶园
West Lake Longjing (Dragon Well) Tea Garden

龙井茶的核心产区集中于浙江杭州的狮峰山、梅家坞、翁家山、云栖、虎跑、灵隐等地，其中以狮峰山龙井茶的品质最高。

　　龙井茶素以"色绿、香郁、味甘、形美"著称于世。通常通过外形、香气、滋味、汤色和叶底五个方面来鉴别龙井茶的品质。外形以扁平光滑、挺秀尖削、均匀整齐、色泽翠绿鲜活的为上品；品质好的龙井茶带有鲜纯的嫩香，香气清醇持久；滋味与香气成正比，香气好的茶叶，通常滋味也好，以鲜醇甘爽为好；汤色主要看色度、亮度和清浊度，以清澈明亮为好；优质的龙井茶叶底芽叶细嫩成朵、大小匀齐、嫩绿明亮。

The Longjing Tea is produced mainly in Mt. Shifeng, Meijiawu, Mt. Wengjia, Yunqi, Hupao, and Lingyin, all in Hangzhou of Zhejiang Province. Among them the highest quality tea is the Longjing Tea from Mt. Shifeng.

　　The Longjing Tea has been known for its green leaves, rich aroma, sweet taste, and beautiful shape. Normally, the quality of the Longjing Tea is judged on five aspects, namely appearance, aroma, taste, soup color, and brewed leaves. The best-quality tea has a flat and smooth appearance, tapering leaves, an even and neat contour, and a fresh green color. The good-quality Longjing Tea has a pure and fresh aroma that lasts long. Its taste is in direct proportion to its aroma. The tea leaves with good aroma usually have good taste. The fresh sweet taste is the best. Tea soup is judged on its tone, brightness, and clearness. The clear and bright tea soup is the best. The high-quality Longjing Tea has tender, complete, green, and bright brewed leaves that are in even sizes.

《茶经》成书于公元750年前后，系统地介绍了唐代及唐代以前的茶叶历史、产地、功效、栽培、采制、煎煮、饮用等知识。

Completed around 750 A.D., The Classic of Tea systematically introduced history, producing origins, efficacy, cultivation, harvesting, processing, brewing/infusing methods and drinking of tea in and before the Tang Dynasty (618—907).

茶經卷上

唐竟陵陸羽鴻漸撰

一之源

茶者南方之嘉木也一尺二尺迺至數十尺其
巴山峽川有兩人合抱者伐而掇之其樹如瓜
蘆葉如梔子花如白薔薇實如栟櫚葉如丁香
根如胡桃

日期 DATE　　　　　天气 WEATHER

时间设定 TIME	计划 TASK	☑ or ☒
		☐
		☐
		☐
		☐
		☐
		☐
		☐

特别提醒 NOTICE

在《茶经》问世之前，茶通常是与饭食同煮的，很少单独饮用。陆羽认为这样的煮法掩盖了茶叶原有的清香味道，于是在《茶经》中提出直接清饮的饮茶方法。

Before The Classic of Tea came out, tea was normally cooked together with rice and other food. It was seldom consumed as a separate drink. Lu Yu believed that such practice concealed tea's natural aroma. He thus recommended direct tea drinking in his work The Classsic of Tea.

日期 DATE　　　　　　天气 WEATHER

时间设定 TIME	计划 TASK	☑ or ☒
		☐
		☐
		☐
		☐
		☐
		☐
		☐

特别提醒 NOTICE

宋代，民间饮茶之风盛行，并逐渐发展出以茶待客的礼仪。

In the Song Dynasty (960–1279), tea drinking was popular among ordinary people. Gradually, the etiquette of treating guests with tea came into being.

日期 DATE   天气 WEATHER

时间设定 TIME	计划 TASK	☑ or ☒

☐

☐

☐

☐

☐

☐

☐

特别提醒 NOTICE

宋代以末茶、散茶为主，但团茶、饼茶依然受到人们的喜爱，而且在蒸压团茶时，会加入龙脑等名贵香料。

In the Song Dynasty (960—1279), dust tea and loose tea were very popular, but lump tea and caky tea were still loved by people. In producing the lump tea, precious spices such as borneol could be mixed in.

日期 DATE　　　　　　　天气 WEATHER

时间设定 TIME	计划 TASK	☑ or ☒
		☐
		☐
		☐
		☐
		☐
		☐
		☐

特别提醒 NOTICE

宋代饮茶方法以点茶为主，即先烤茶饼，再敲碎，碾成细末，用茶笰将茶末筛细。茶末放于碗中，倒入少量沸水调成糊状。用釜烧水，微沸初漾时，即将开水冲入杯、盏、碗内。

The process of drinking tea was breaking the baked cake tea and then shifting the ground small with tea sieve, putting the tea powder in a bowl or cup and mixing with small amount of hot water to get a paste, boiling water in a kettle, then infusing the boiling water into the bowl or cup as soon as the water just started boil.

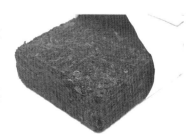

日期 DATE   天气 WEATHER

时间设定 TIME	计划 TASK	☑ or ☒
		☐
		☐
		☐
		☐
		☐
		☐
		☐

特别提醒 NOTICE

明清时期逐渐废除了饼茶进贡，流行炒制散茶，其冲饮方法也与此前有了很大的不同，改煮为泡，直接将一小撮茶叶放入茶杯或茶壶，倒入开水即成。

In the Ming Dynasty (1368—1644) and the Qing Dynasty (1644—1911), caky tea was gradually abolished as tribute. Instead, loose tea production was popular. Its making and drinking methods were quite different from the previous ones. Boiling was replaced by brewing. A pinch of tea leaves was put into a tea cup or teapot and boiling water was poured in to make tea.

日期 DATE   天气 WEATHER

时间设定 TIME	计划 TASK	☑ or ☒
		☐
		☐
		☐
		☐
		☐
		☐
		☐

特别提醒 NOTICE

现代，中国人饮茶的主要方式是清饮法，即以开水直接冲泡茶叶的方法。除此之外，也出现了一些新的内容和形式，如调饮法、袋泡茶、听装茶等。

In modern times, Chinese people drink tea by brewing tea leaves directly with boiling water. There are also other new contents and forms of tea drinking, including tea flavoring method, bag tea, and canned tea.

日期 DATE　　　　　　　天气 WEATHER

时间设定 TIME	计划 TASK	☑ or ☒
		☐
		☐
		☐
		☐
		☐
		☐
		☐

特别提醒 NOTICE

茶俗是指在长期的社会生活中，逐渐形成的一种以茶为主题或是以茶为媒介的风俗习惯。

Tea custom refers to the social custom and habits focusing on tea or carried on by tea that have gradually taken shaped during the long-term social life.

日期 DATE　　　　　　　天气 WEATHER

时间设定 TIME	计划 TASK	☑ or ☒
		☐
		☐
		☐
		☐
		☐
		☐
		☐

特别提醒 NOTICE

洞庭山碧螺春茶园
Biluochun (Green Spiral Spring) Tea Garden on Mt. Dongting

洞庭山，位于江苏苏州的太湖之滨，这里茶园遍布，各种果树遍插其间，以生产中国十大历史传统名茶之一的洞庭碧螺春而名扬四海。

碧螺春茶以形美、色艳、香浓、味醇"四绝"闻名中外。其品质特点是：条索纤细，卷曲成螺，披毫隐翠，香气浓郁，滋味鲜醇甘厚，汤色碧绿清澈，叶底嫩绿明亮。另外，由于碧螺春茶树与桃树、李树、杏树、梅树、石榴等果木交错种植，茶树、果树枝桠相连，根脉相通，使得茶吸果香，花窖茶味，遂有了碧螺春茶所特有的花香果味的品质特点。

Mt. Dongting stands by the Taihu Lake beside Suzhou of Jiangsu Province. It is full of tea gardens and various fruit trees and is well known for its production of the Biluochun Tea, one of the top ten famous historical teas of China.

The Biluochun Tea is well-known at home and abroad for its four extreme beauties, namely shape, color, aroma, and taste. The tea strips are thin and curl up as spirals. Its green color is obscured by its apparent tips. The tea has strong aroma and fresh and sweet taste. The tea soup is green and clear and the brewed tea leaves are tenderly green and bright. In addition, as the Biluochun tea trees are planted amidst several fruit trees such as peach tree, plum tree, apricot tree, prune tree, and pomegranate tree, their branches get intertwined and the Biluochun Tea absorbs the fruit scent and flower fragrance.

中国传统茶俗根据实际情况的不同可分为日常饮茶、客来敬茶、婚恋用茶、祭祀供茶等。

Traditional tea custom of China vary with actual conditions and can be divided into daily tea drinking, guest entertainment with tea, tea consumption during marriage arrangement and wedding, and sacrifice offering with tea.

日期 DATE   天气 WEATHER

时间设定 TIME	计划 TASK	☑ or ☒
		☐
		☐
		☐
		☐
		☐
		☐
		☐

特别提醒 NOTICE

以茶敬客之风最早出现于魏晋南北朝时期，唐宋时期普及开来。当客人来访时，为客人端上一杯香茶以示尊重和欢迎。

Tea was first offered to the guests in the Wei, Jin, and Northern and Southern Dynasties (420–589). Such custom became a popular practice in the Tang (618–907) and the Song (960–1279) dynasties. When a guest comes, the host offers tea to him as a gesture of respect and welcome.

日期 DATE　　　　　　　天气 WEATHER

时间设定 TIME	计划 TASK	☑ or ☒
		☐
		☐
		☐
		☐
		☐
		☐
		☐

特别提醒 NOTICE

婚恋用茶是指在婚恋的过程中茶的使用形式，有定亲茶、受聘茶、新娘子茶，这些用茶形式在中国少数民族中最为常见。

Tea consumption during marriage arrangement and wedding includes engagement tea and bridal tea, which are the commonest ways of tea using among the minority ethnic groups of China.

日期 DATE   天气 WEATHER

时间设定 TIME	计划 TASK	☑ or ☒
		☐
		☐
		☐
		☐
		☐
		☐
		☐

特别提醒 NOTICE

祭祀供茶在中国有着悠久的历史，有三种常见的方式：一是在茶碗或茶盏中注上茶水用来祭祀，二是只用干茶祭祀，三是只用茶壶、茶盅等茶具作为祭祀用品。

Tea has long been used as a sacrifice item in China. There are three ways of offering tea as a sacrifice. The first is to offer tea water contained in a tea bowl or a tea cup as a sacrifice. The second is to offer dry tea as a sacrifice. The third is to present tea sets such as teapot and tea cup as a way of sacrifice offering.

日期 DATE　　　　　　天气 WEATHER

时间设定 TIME	计划 TASK	☑ or ☒

☐

☐

☐

☐

☐

☐

☐

特别提醒 NOTICE

绿茶，是人类制茶史上出现最早的加工茶，属于不发酵茶。其最显著的特征是清汤绿叶，即干茶色泽翠绿，茶汤黄绿明亮，叶底（茶渣）鲜绿。

Green tea is the earliest unfermented tea processed by human. Its most obvious features are the clear tea water and green leaves. The dry tea leaves are green and the tea water is bright yellowish green. The brewed tea leaves (tea dregs) are fresh green.

日期 DATE　　　　　　　　天气 WEATHER

时间设定 TIME	计划 TASK	☑ or ☒
		☐
		☐
		☐
		☐
		☐
		☐
		☐

特别提醒 NOTICE

绿茶的品种最多、产量最高、产区最广，几乎中国的各产茶区均产绿茶。

The green tea has the most varieties. Its output is the highest among all teas. It is produced in the widest areas. Almost all tea—producing areas in China produce green tea.

日期 DATE   天气 WEATHER

时间设定 TIME	计划 TASK	☑ or ☒
		☐
		☐
		☐
		☐
		☐
		☐
		☐

特别提醒 NOTICE

绿茶制作一般经过杀青、揉捻、干燥三道工序。其中杀青是决定绿茶色泽的关键工序，即以高温使叶中水分蒸发，青臭气发散出去，以产生茶香。

Producing green tea normally goes through three processing procedures: fixation, rolling, and drying. Among them, fixation is the key procedure to decide the color of the green tea. During fixation, high temperature is applied to make the tea leaves dehydrated and their green odor is dispersed. As a result, tea aroma is created.

时间设定 TIME	计划 TASK	☑ or ☒
		☐
		☐
		☐
		☐
		☐
		☐
		☐

特别提醒 NOTICE

冲泡绿茶一般选用容水量在100毫升～150毫升的玻璃杯，茶叶的投放量为2克～5克，冲入开水150毫升左右。

The green tea is normally brewed in a 100ml to 150ml glass. Put two to five grams of tea leaves into the glass and pour in 150ml boiling water.

日期 DATE   天气 WEATHER

时间设定 TIME	计划 TASK	☑ or ☒
		☐
		☐
		☐
		☐
		☐
		☐
		☐

特别提醒 NOTICE

黄山毛峰茶山

Maofeng (Hairy Tip) Tea Mountain on Mt. Huangshan

黄山毛峰前身叫"云雾茶"，因该茶白毫披身，芽尖似峰，故得名"毛峰"，后再冠以地名为"黄山毛峰"。黄山毛峰是条形烘青绿茶。从清明到立夏均为采摘期，特级黄山毛峰的采摘标准为一芽一叶初展。采来的芽头和鲜叶要进行选剔，使芽叶匀齐一致。黄山毛峰成茶外形似雀舌，白毫显露，色如象牙，鱼叶金黄。冲泡后汤色清澈，滋味鲜浓、醇厚甘甜，叶底嫩黄，肥壮成朵。泡好的黄山毛峰芽叶直竖悬浮，继而徐徐下沉，即使茶凉后，仍有余香，人称"冷香"。

The Maofeng Tea from Mt. Huangshan used to be called the Yunwu (Cloud and Mist) Tea. This tea has white tips and peak-like buds, hence its name Maofeng (hairy tip in Chinese). Adding the name of its producing place, it is called Huangshan Maofeng Tea. The Maofeng Tea from Mt. Huangshan is a baked green tea in strip shape. It is picked during the period from Pure Brightness to the Beginning of Summer. The superfine Huangshan Maofeng is picked when the first bud and leaf begin to open. The picked buds and fresh leaves should be carefully sorted out to make them even and consistent with each other. The baked Huangshan Maofeng Tea has the shape of a sparrow's tongue, exposed white tips, the color of the ivory, and golden leaves. The tea soup is clear and tastes fresh and sweet. The brewed tea leaves are yellow and fat and cluster into lumps. After thorough brewing, the tea leaves first stand vertically in the water and then slowly sink. Even when the tea water gets cold, it keeps the aroma, known as cold aroma.

绿茶中的名品主要有西湖龙井、洞庭山碧螺春、庐山云雾茶、黄山毛峰、太平猴魁、峨眉竹叶青、信阳毛尖茶、顾渚紫笋茶、普陀佛茶、安吉白茶等。

There are many famous green tea varieties, including the West Lake Longjing Tea, Biluochun Tea from Mt. Dongting, Yunwu Tea from Mt. Lushan, Maofeng Tea from Mt. Huangshan, Houkui Tea from Taiping, Zhuyeqing Tea from Mt. Emei, Maojian Tea from Xinyang, Zisun Tea from Mt. Guzhu, Buddha Tea from Mt. Putuo, and Anji White Tea.

日期 DATE   天气 WEATHER

时间设定 TIME	计划 TASK	☑ or ☒
		☐
		☐
		☐
		☐
		☐
		☐
		☐

特别提醒 NOTICE

龙井茶素以"色绿、香郁、味甘、形美"著称于世，被誉为"天下第一名茶"。

The Longjing Tea which is hailed the No.1 Tea in the world, has been known for its green leaves, rich aroma, sweet taste, and beautiful shape.

时间设定 TIME	计划 TASK	☑ or ☒
		☐
		☐
		☐
		☐
		☐
		☐
		☐

特别提醒 NOTICE

龙井茶的采摘要求是"早、嫩、勤"。其中,"早"是指采摘的时间,清明前采制的龙井茶品质最佳,称"明前茶",谷雨前采摘的品质尚好,称"雨前茶"。

Picking of the Longjing Tea focuses on three elements, namely Early Picking, Picking of Tender Leaves, and Thorough Picking. The tea picked before the Qingming Festival, or Pure Brightness, one of the 24 solar terms in Chinese lunar calendar, has the best quality and is called Pre—PB tea.

日期 DATE   天气 WEATHER

时间设定 TIME	计划 TASK	☑ or ☒
		☐
		☐
		☐
		☐
		☐
		☐
		☐

特别提醒 NOTICE

顾渚山位于浙江省湖州市长兴县西北部，属水口乡顾渚村，产茶历史悠久，出产的紫笋茶最为著名。顾渚山紫笋茶因芽叶微紫、嫩叶背卷似笋壳而得名。

Mt. Guzhu stands in the northwest of Changxing County, Huzhou City, Zhejiang Province. The area belongs to Guzhu Village of Shuikou Township. Tea has long been produced here. Among the local teas, the Zisun Tea is the most famous. The Zisun Tea from Mt. Guzhu derives its name from its purple buds and leaves and bamboo—shoot—like backward rolling tender leaves.

日期 DATE   天气 WEATHER

时间设定 TIME	计划 TASK	☑ or ☒
		☐
		☐
		☐
		☐
		☐
		☐
		☐

特别提醒 NOTICE

早在唐代，顾渚山紫笋茶就成为皇家贡茶的"最爱"，后历朝续贡达876年。

As far back as the Tang Dynasty (618–907), the Zisun Tea from Mt. Guzhu had been the favorite tribute tea of the royal family. It remained a tribute tea for 876 years through the following dynasties.

日期 DATE　　　　　　　天气 WEATHER

时间设定 TIME	计划 TASK	☑ or ☒
		☐
		☐
		☐
		☐
		☐
		☐
		☐

特别提醒 NOTICE

顾渚紫笋茶在唐时是饼茶，宋时为龙团茶，明后改以芽茶进贡。

The Zisun Tea was a caky tea in the Tang Dynasty (618 – 907), a dragon lump tea in the Song Dynasty (960–1279), and a bud tea since the Ming Dynasty (1368–1644).

日期 DATE   天气 WEATHER

时间设定 TIME	计划 TASK	☑ or ☒

☐

☐

☐

☐

☐

☐

☐

特别提醒 NOTICE

顾渚紫笋是半烘炒型绿茶，于清明前至谷雨期间采摘，标准为一芽一叶或一芽二叶初展。

The Zisun Tea from Mt. Guzhu is a semi-baked and semi-stirfixation green tea. It is picked and made during the period between Pure Brightness and Grain Rain when one bud with one leaf or one bud with two leaves begin to open.

日期 DATE　　　　　　　天气 WEATHER

时间设定 TIME	计划 TASK	☑ or ☒
		☐
		☐
		☐
		☐
		☐
		☐
		☐

特别提醒 NOTICE

顾渚紫笋的成茶芽挺叶长，形似兰花，色泽翠绿，银毫明显，冲泡后汤色清澈明亮，滋味甘醇鲜爽，叶底细嫩成朵。

The mature tea of Zisun Tea from Mt. Guzhu has long buds and leaves which are shaped like orchid in bright green and with obvious silver tips. The tea soup is bright and clear, with a sweet and fresh taste. The brewed tea leaves are tender and cluster into lumps.

时间设定 TIME	计划 TASK	☑ or ☒
		☐
		☐
		☐
		☐
		☐
		☐
		☐

特别提醒 NOTICE

君山银针茶的品饮

The Tasting and Drinking of Yinzhen (Silver Tip) Tea from Mt. Junshan

君山是湖南岳阳市洞庭湖中的一座小岛，四面环水，风光独好。君山产茶，有史可查的始于唐代，因茶叶满披茸毛，底色泛黄，冲泡后像黄色羽毛一样竖立起来，一度被称为"黄翎毛"。君山银针茶始于唐代，相传文成公主出嫁西藏时就选带了君山茶。君山茶在清朝时被列为贡茶。

　　君山银针以色、香、味、形俱佳而著称。制成的茶芽壮挺直，长短大小均匀，内呈橙黄色，外裹一层白毫，故有"金镶玉"之称，又因茶芽外形像银针，故名"君山银针"。冲泡后的茶叶全部冲向上面，继而徐徐下沉，三起三落。茶汤色泽杏黄明亮，饮之味醇干爽，茶香四溢，叶底黄亮匀齐。

Mt. Junshan is a small isle in the Dongting Lake of Yueyang City, which is surrounded by water on four sides and has a beautiful landscape. Tea has been produced in Mt. Junshan since the Tang Dynasty (618 – 907). The tea leaves are covered with hairs on a yellow background. After brewing, they stand up in the water like yellow plumes, hence its another name Huanglingmao (Yellow Plume) in history. The Yinzhen Tea from Mt. Junshan started in the Tang Dynasty . According to the legend, when Princess Wen Cheng was married to the King of Tibet, she took with her the tea from Mt. Junshan. The Junshan Tea was chosen as a tribute tea in the Qing Dynasty (1644 – 1911).

The Yinzhen Tea from Mt. Junshan is known for its color, aroma, taste, and appearance. The tea bud is thick and straight with even length and size. With an orange interior, it is covered with a layer of white hairs. It is therefore known as "Jade with God Inlay". As the tea bud looks like a silver needle, it is formally called Junshan Yinzhen. After brewing, the tea leaves first float on the surface and then slowly sink. This process goes on for three rounds. The tea soup is apricot yellow and bright and tastes mellow and brisk. The tea aroma is profound and spreads far and wide. The brewed tea leaves are yellow, bright, and even.

普陀佛茶是半烘炒绿茶，每年清明后开始采摘，仅采一季春茶。其产区遍及普陀茶山及周围朱家尖、桃花岛等地。

The Buddha Tea from Mt. Putuo is a semi-baked and semi-stirfixation green tea. It is picked once a year in spring after the Pure Brightness. The producing area in Mt. Putuo includes the mountain itself and the neighboring places such as Zhujiajian and Taohua Island.

时间设定 TIME	计划 TASK	☑ or ☒
		☐
		☐
		☐
		☐
		☐
		☐
		☐

特别提醒 NOTICE

普陀佛茶的鲜叶标准为一芽一叶或一芽二叶，成茶外形紧细卷曲，色泽绿润显毫。

The fresh leaves of Buddha Tea from Mt. Putuo present a shape of one bud with one bud with two leaves. It has tightly curled leaves with a green, moist, and tippy appearance.

日期 DATE　　　　　　　天气 WEATHER

时间设定 TIME	计划 TASK	☑ or ☒
		☐
		☐
		☐
		☐
		☐
		☐
		☐

特别提醒 NOTICE

普陀佛茶冲泡后汤色黄绿明亮，气味清香高雅，滋味清醇爽口，叶底软亮成朵。

The tea soup of Buddha Tea from Mt. Putuo is bright yellowish green with pleasant sweet aroma. It tastes fresh and pure. The brewed tea leaves are soft and bright and cluster into lumps.

日期 DATE   天气 WEATHER

时间设定 TIME	计划 TASK	☑ or ☒

□

□

□

□

□

□

□

特别提醒 NOTICE

洞庭碧螺春在宋代已经成为贡茶。碧螺春在每年3月18日前后开采，谷雨前结束，以春分至清明采制的明前茶品质最为上等。

The Biluochun from Mt. Dongting had been made a tribute tea since the Song Dynasty (960—1279). The Biluochun Tea is picked from March 18 to the end of Grain Rain each year. The Pre-PB pickings from the Spring Equinox to Pure Brightness have the best quality.

日期 DATE   天气 WEATHER

时间设定 TIME	计划 TASK	☑ or ☒

☐

☐

☐

☐

☐

☐

☐

特别提醒 NOTICE

碧螺春通常采一芽一叶初展，形似雀舌，采回的芽叶不能放置，须及时进行精心挑拣，以保持芽叶匀整一致。

Normally, the Biluochun tea leaves with one bud and one leaf are picked when they begin to open in the shape of a sparrow's tongue. The picked buds and leaves should not be left unprocessed. They should be timely and meticulously sorted out to keep the buds and leaves in the same size and shape.

日期 DATE　　　　　　　　天气 WEATHER

时间设定 TIME	计划 TASK	☑ or ☒
		☐
		☐
		☐
		☐
		☐
		☐
		☐

特别提醒 NOTICE

黄山毛峰是条形烘青绿茶。成茶外形似雀舌，白毫显露，色如象牙；冲泡后汤色清澈，滋味鲜浓。

The Maofeng Tea from Mt. Huangshan is a baked green tea in strip shape. The mature Huangshan Maofeng Tea has the shape of a sparrow's tongue, exposed white tips, the color of the ivory leaves. The tea soup is clear and tastes fresh.

日期 DATE　　　　　　　天气 WEATHER

时间设定 TIME	计划 TASK	☑ or ☒
		☐
		☐
		☐
		☐
		☐
		☐
		☐

特别提醒 NOTICE

庐山云雾茶的前身庐山茶，为东晋时古刹名寺的僧侣所创制。到唐代时，庐山茶已很著名，云雾茶之名则是出现在明代《庐山志》之中。

The Yunwu Tea from Mt. Lushan was known as Lushan Tea before. It was planted and made by monks of the temples in the Eastern Jin Dynasty (317—420).By the Tang Dynasty (618—907), the Lushan Tea had been very famous. The Yunwu Tea appeared in the Chronicles of Mt. Lushan in the Ming Dynasty (1368—1644).

时间设定 TIME	计划 TASK	☑ or ☒
		☐
		☐
		☐
		☐
		☐
		☐
		☐

特别提醒 NOTICE

1964年4月，陈毅副总理途经四川峨眉山万年寺。万年寺方丈用新采制的绿茶奉送给陈毅副总理品尝。陈毅副总理饮后顿觉清香沁脾，在得知此茶尚未取名时，见此茶形、色似竹叶，且清香宜人，便为之取名"竹叶青"。

In April 1964, vice premier Chen Yi arrived in Sichuan and took a rest at the Wannian Temple in Mt. Emei. Abbot of the temple presented the newly-made green tea to him. The tea was a good refreshment and vice premier Chen Yi liked it very much. When he was told that the tea was yet to be named, he called it Zhuyeqing because the tea had the shape and color of a bamboo leaf (Zhu: bamboo; Ye: leaf; Qing: green).

日期 DATE 天气 WEATHER

时间设定 TIME	计划 TASK	☑ or ☒
		☐
		☐
		☐
		☐
		☐
		☐
		☐

特别提醒 NOTICE

普洱茶山
The Pu'er Tea Mountain

在美丽的云南西双版纳州，有 6 处连片的山岭，合称为"六大茶山"，这便是普洱茶的原产地。云南是茶的发源地之一，早在 3000 多年前就已经开始人工种植茶树。到唐朝时，普洱茶才开始大规模地种植和生产，那时称为"普茶"。清朝时，普洱茶达到鼎盛，并被列为贡茶，也常常作为国礼赠送给外国使节。

　　普洱茶最根本的品质特征在于耐久。茶叶一般来说以新鲜为好，但普洱茶可以在自然中呼吸，在空气中持续发酵，存放越久，茶香越醇。普洱茶的香气高锐持久，带有云南大叶种茶的独特香型，滋味浓烈，富于刺激性；芽壮叶厚，白毫密布，经五六次冲泡后仍持有香味，汤色橙黄浓郁。

There are six integrated mountains in the beautiful Xishuangbanna Prefecture of Yunnan. Known as "the Six Major Tea Mountains", they are the place of origin of the Pu' er Tea. Yunnan is one of the birthplaces of tea. People began planting tea trees in Yunnan over 3,000 years ago. By the Tang Dynasty (618 – 907), the Pu' er Tea had been under large-scale planting and production. It was called Pu Tea at that time. In the Qing Dynasty (1644 – 1911), the Pu' er Tea reached its zenith and was chosen as a tribute tea and a national gift for foreign envoys.

　　The most fundamental feature of the Pu' er Tea is its endurance. Normally, fresh tea is better than the old one. However, the Pu' er Tea can breathe in a natural environment and keep on fermentation in the air. The longer it is stored, the mellower it becomes. The Pu' er Tea has a strong and long-lasting aroma, the one peculiar to Yunnan bigleaved tea. Its taste is strong. It has sturdy buds and thick leaves covered with white hairs. After five or six rounds of brewing, its aroma still remains. The tea soup is orange and thick.

竹叶青茶鲜叶一般在清明前3～5天开采，标准为一芽一叶或一芽二叶初展，芽叶嫩匀，大小一致。

The fresh leaves of the Zhuyeqing Tea are normally picked three to five days before Pure Brightness. The picking is done when the first bud and first leaf or the first bud and first two leaves begin to open. The buds and leaves should be tender and even and in the same size.

日期 DATE　　　　　　　　天气 WEATHER

时间设定 TIME	计划 TASK	☑ or ☒
		☐
		☐
		☐
		☐
		☐
		☐
		☐

特别提醒 NOTICE

竹叶青成品茶外形扁平光滑，两头尖细，形似竹叶，颜色翠绿，冲泡后汤色青澄，滋味浓醇，叶底嫩绿均匀。

The baked Zhuyeqing Tea has a flat and smooth appearance. Its two ends are green and tapering like a bamboo leaf. The tea soup is green and clear with a rich flavor. The brewed tea leaves are tender, green, and even.

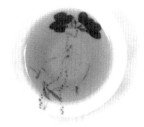

日期 DATE   天气 WEATHER

时间设定 TIME	计划 TASK	☑ or ☒
		☐
		☐
		☐
		☐
		☐
		☐
		☐

特别提醒 NOTICE

黄茶属于轻发酵茶，品质特点为黄叶黄汤、香气清悦、味厚爽口，主产于浙江、四川、安徽、湖南、广东、湖北等省。

The yellow tea is a slightly-fermented tea featuring yellow leaves, yellow tea soup, clear and pleasant aroma, and strong and brisk taste. It is mainly produced in Zhejiang, Sichuan, Anhui, Hunan, Guangdong, and Hubei.

日期 DATE   天气 WEATHER

时间设定 TIME	计划 TASK	☑ or ☒

☐

☐

☐

☐

☐

☐

☐

特别提醒 NOTICE

冲泡黄茶时，投茶量与绿茶相同，冲泡时水温以70℃为宜。

In yellow tea brewing, the amount of the tea leaves applied is equivalent to that of the green tea. The best water temperature for brewing is 70 ℃ .

时间设定 TIME	计划 TASK	☑ or ☒
		☐
		☐
		☐
		☐
		☐
		☐
		☐

特别提醒 NOTICE

黄茶与绿茶制作工艺相似，主要品种包括君山银针、蒙顶黄芽、莫干黄芽等。

The yellow tea is produced in the similar process with the green tea. Main varieties of this tea include Junshan Yinzhen (Silver Tip), Mengding Huangya, and Mogan Huangya.

日期 DATE   天气 WEATHER

时间设定 TIME   计划 TASK   ☑ or ☒

☐

☐

☐

☐

☐

☐

☐

特别提醒 NOTICE

蒙山蒙顶茶自唐开始作为贡茶，一直延续到清代，长达1000余年。

The Mengding Tea from Mt. Mengshan served as a tribute tea for over 1,000 years from the Tang Dynasty (618–907) to the Qing Dynasty (1644–1911).

时间设定 TIME	计划 TASK	☑ or ☒
		☐
		☐
		☐
		☐
		☐
		☐
		☐

特别提醒 NOTICE

蒙顶茶中最著名的是蒙顶甘露和蒙顶黄芽。蒙顶甘露属炒青绿茶，外形紧卷多毫，汤色清澈微黄。蒙顶黄芽为黄茶类茶中珍品，外形扁直，汤色黄亮。

Among many Mengding teas, the most famous are Mengding Ganlu (Sweet Dew) and Mengding Huangya (Yellow Bud). The Mengding Ganlu is a stir fixation green tea. It is twisted and tippy and the tea soup is clear with a yellowish tint. The Mengding Huangya is a top-grade product among yellow teas. It has a flat contour and the tea soup is brightly yellow.

日期 DATE   天气 WEATHER

时间设定 TIME	计划 TASK	☑ or ☒
		☐
		☐
		☐
		☐
		☐
		☐
		☐

特别提醒 NOTICE

君山银针茶始于唐代，相传文成公主出嫁西藏时就选带了君山茶。君山茶在清朝时被列为贡茶。

The Yinzhen Tea from Mt. Junshan started in the Tang Dynasty (618—907). According to the legend, when Princess Wen Cheng was married to the King of Tibet, she took with her the tea from Mt. Junshan. The Junshan Tea was chosen as a tribute tea in the Qing Dynasty (1644—1911).

日期 DATE　　　　　　　天气 WEATHER

时间设定 TIME	计划 TASK	☑ or ☒
		☐
		☐
		☐
		☐
		☐
		☐
		☐

特别提醒 NOTICE

武夷山大红袍茶园
Wuyi Dahongpao Tea garden

武夷山位于福建省武夷山市境内，悬崖绝壁，深坑巨谷。先人利用岩凹、石隙、石缝，沿边砌筑石岸，并在其中栽茶，产有"四大名丛"：大红袍、水金龟、白鸡冠、铁罗汉。人们将这些产于武夷山的乌龙茶称为"武夷岩茶"，其中尤以大红袍为贵，称其为武夷岩茶中的"王中之王"。大红袍品质很有特色，成茶条紧，色泽绿褐，冲泡后的汤色橙黄，香气馥郁，具有持久的桂花香，这种韵味为大红袍所特有。乌龙茶通常能冲泡三四次；名丛能冲泡五六次，好的能做到"七泡有余香"；而大红袍甚至冲至八九次，仍不脱原茶真味桂花香。

Mt. Wuyi which has precipitous cliffs, deep pits, and huge valleys, stands in the territory of Wuyishan City of Fujian Province. The ancient people planted tea trees in the rock pits, crevices, and cracks by building embankment with rocks. There are top four Mingcongs: Dahongpao (Big Red Robe), Shuijingui (Water Golden Turtle), Baijiguan (White Comb), and Tieluohan (Iron Arhat). People call the oolong tea produced in Mt. Wuyi the Wuyi Rock Tea, among which, Dahongpao is the best and it is called the king of kings of the Wuyi Rock Tea. Dahongpao has a unique quality. The finished tea is seen as tight and greenish brown strips. The orange tea soup sends forth strong aroma, like the lasting fragrance of sweetscented osmanthus. Such taste is peculiar to Dahongpao. The Oolong Tea can last three to four rounds of brewing. The Mingcong can last five to six rounds. The high-quality one still has aroma even after seven rounds of brewing. Dahongpao, however, can last eight to nine rounds of brewing and still keep its fragrance. It is indeed the King of Teas.

君山银针以色、香、味、形俱佳而著称。成品茶芽头茁壮直，长短大小均匀，芽内面呈金黄色，外裹一层白毫，故有"金镶玉"之称。

The Yinzhen Tea from Mt. Junshan is known for its color, aroma, taste, and appearance. The baked tea bud is thick and straight with even length and size. With an orange interior, it is covered with a layer of white hairs. It is therefore known as "Jade with God Inlay".

日期 DATE　　　　　　天气 WEATHER

时间设定 TIME	计划 TASK	☑ or ☒

特别提醒 NOTICE

黑茶属后发酵茶，是中国特有的茶类。其所用原料较粗老，制造过程中堆积发酵时间较长，是一种成茶色泽油黑或黑褐色的茶种。

The dark tea is a post-fermented tea, a unique tea variety of China. It is made with coarse and old raw materials through a long period of piled fermentation. The baked tea is oily black or blackish brown.

日期 DATE　　　　　　　天气 WEATHER

时间设定 TIME	计划 TASK	☑ or ☒

☐

☐

☐

☐

☐

☐

☐

特别提醒 NOTICE

黑茶质地较为坚硬，为了使茶叶中的营养成分充分溶解，一般采用壶泡的方式，且宜用现沸的开水冲泡，茶叶的投放量以壶容量的三四成为好。

The dark tea has a hard texture. To fully dissolve the nutrients in the tea leaves, teapot brewing is usually adopted and the fresh boiling water is used. The tea leaves applied should occupy three or four tenths of the teapot volume.

日期 DATE   天气 WEATHER

时间设定 TIME	计划 TASK	☑ or ☒

☐

☐

☐

☐

☐

☐

☐

特别提醒 NOTICE

黑茶的主要品种有云南的普洱茶、湖南的黑毛茶、湖北的老青茶、四川的南路边茶与西路边茶、广西的六堡茶等，其中以云南的普洱茶最负盛名。

Among the major dark teas are the Pu' er Tea of Yunnan, Heimao (Black Hair) Tea of Hunan, Laoqing (Old Black) Tea of Hubei, Nanlubian (Southern Roadside) Tea and Xilubian (Western Roadside) Tea of Sichuan, and Liubao (Six-castle) Tea of Guangxi. The Pu'er Tea of Yunnan is the most famous.

日期 DATE　　　　　　　天气 WEATHER

时间设定 TIME	计划 TASK	☑ or ☒
		☐
		☐
		☐
		☐
		☐
		☐
		☐

特别提醒 NOTICE

普洱茶属云南大叶种茶，最根本的品质特征在于耐久。

The Pu'er Tea is a kind of Yunnan big-leaved tea and its most fundamental feature is endurance.

日期 DATE   天气 WEATHER

时间设定 TIME	计划 TASK	☑ or ☒
		☐
		☐
		☐
		☐
		☐
		☐
		☐

特别提醒 NOTICE

白茶是一种轻微发酵茶，因其表面披满白色茸毛而得名，主要品种有白毫银针、白牡丹、贡眉等。

The white tea is a slightly-fermented tea. It derives its name from the white hairs on its surface. Major white tea varieties include White-tipped Yinzhen, Baimudan (White Peony), and Gongmei.

日期 DATE　　　　　　　天气 WEATHER

时间设定 TIME	计划 TASK	☑ or ☒
		☐
		☐
		☐
		☐
		☐
		☐
		☐

特别提醒 NOTICE

冲泡白茶，茶叶的投放量与绿茶相当，每克茶的用水量约为50毫升。白茶的茶汁不易浸出，冲泡时间较长，适宜煎服。

In white tea brewing, the amount of the tea leaves applied is equivalent to that of the green tea. For each gram of tea, about 50ml water should be used. The taste of the white tea is harder to get loose and thus it requires longer period of brewing. Cooking can be a proper choice.

时间设定 TIME	计划 TASK	☑ or ☒
		☐
		☐
		☐
		☐
		☐
		☐
		☐

特别提醒 NOTICE

乌龙茶，即青茶，属半发酵茶，是中国独具特色的茶叶品类，名品有武夷山大红袍、安溪铁观音、凤凰山单丛茶、台湾冻顶乌龙茶等。

The Oolong Tea is a semi-fermented tea, a unique tea variety of China. Among the famous Oolong teas are the Dahongpao from Mt. Wuyi, Anxi Tieguanyin (Iron Goddess of Mercy), Dancong Tea from Mt. Phoenix, and Dongding Oolong Tea from Taiwan.

日期 DATE　　　　　　　　天气 WEATHER

时间设定 TIME	计划 TASK	☑ or ☒
		☐
		☐
		☐
		☐
		☐
		☐
		☐

特别提醒 NOTICE

乌龙茶的冲泡是最为讲究、最为复杂的。一般冲泡乌龙茶，宜选用紫砂壶，同时根据品饮人数选用大小适宜的壶。

Brewing of the Oolong Tea requires the best-planned and most complicated procedures. Normally, the purple sand teapot is the best for brewing the Oolong Tea. The size of the teapot is chosen based on the number of the drinkers.

日期 DATE　　　　　　　天气 WEATHER

时间设定 TIME	计划 TASK	☑ or ☒
		☐
		☐
		☐
		☐
		☐
		☐
		☐

特别提醒 NOTICE

安溪铁观音又名"红心观音",是用铁观音茶树鲜叶为原料制成的乌龙茶,冲泡后汤色金黄,浓艳似琥珀,有天然馥郁的兰花香。

Also known as Hongxin Guanyin (Red-heart Goddess of Mercy) and Hongyang Guanyin (Redappearance Goddess of Mercy), Anxi Tieguanyin is a kind of Oolong tea made with the fresh leaves of the Tieguanyin tea trees. The tea soup is golden as amber and sends forth natural rich orchid fragrance.

时间设定 TIME	计划 TASK	☑ or ☒
		☐
		☐
		☐
		☐
		☐
		☐
		☐

特别提醒 NOTICE

红茶属于全发酵茶类，因其干茶色泽和冲泡的茶汤以红色为主而得名。

Black tea is fully fermented tea and its name comes from the red color of the dry tea and the brewed tea soup.

日期 DATE   天气 WEATHER

时间设定 TIME	计划 TASK	☑ or ☒

☐

☐

☐

☐

☐

☐

☐

特别提醒 NOTICE

红茶的鼻祖在中国，世界上最早的红茶由中国福建武夷山茶区的茶农发明。中国红茶种类较多，包括祁门红茶、工夫红茶和小种红茶等。

Black tea originated from China and the world's first black tea was invented by farmers in Wuyishan of Fujian Province in China. Among the major black teas are the Keemun Black Tea, Congou Black Tea, and Souchong, etc.

日期 DATE   天气 WEATHER

时间设定 TIME	计划 TASK	☑ or ☒

☐

☐

☐

☐

☐

☐

☐

特别提醒 NOTICE

冲泡红茶有两种方法：清饮泡法和调饮泡法。清饮泡法每克茶用水量以50毫升～60毫升为宜；调饮泡法是在茶汤中加入糖、牛奶、蜂蜜、柠檬等调料，茶叶的投放量可随品饮者的口味而定。

There are two ways to brew the black tea: brewing pure tea and brewing laced tea. To brew pure tea, each gram of tea leaves needs 50ml to 60ml water. To brew laced tea, the condiments such as sugar, milk, honey, and lemon juice are added into the tea soup. The quantity of the tea leaves depends on the taste of the drinker.

日期 DATE　　　　　　　　天气 WEATHER

时间设定 TIME	计划 TASK	☑ or ☒
		☐
		☐
		☐
		☐
		☐
		☐
		☐

特别提醒 NOTICE

祁门红茶具有香高、色艳、味醇的特点，冲泡时水温以90℃为宜，多采用白瓷杯冲泡。

The Keemun Black Tea features high aroma, bright color, and mellow taste. The best brewing temperature is 90℃ . Normally, white porcelain teacup is used.

名字 NAME

手机 CELLPHONE

电话 PHONE

邮箱 E-MAIL

地址 ADDRESS

名字 NAME

手机 CELLPHONE

电话 PHONE

邮箱 E-MAIL

地址 ADDRESS

名字 NAME

手机 CELLPHONE

电话 PHONE

邮箱 E-MAIL

地址 ADDRESS

名字 NAME

手机 CELLPHONE

电话 PHONE

邮箱 E-MAIL

地址 ADDRESS

名字 NAME

手机 CELLPHONE

电话 PHONE

邮箱 E-MAIL

地址 ADDRESS

名字 NAME

手机 CELLPHONE

电话 PHONE

邮箱 E-MAIL

地址 ADDRESS

名字 NAME

手机 CELLPHONE

电话 PHONE

邮箱 E-MAIL

地址 ADDRESS

名字 NAME

手机 CELLPHONE

电话 PHONE

邮箱 E-MAIL

地址 ADDRESS

名字 NAME

手机 CELLPHONE

电话 PHONE

邮箱 E-MAIL

地址 ADDRESS

名字 NAME

手机 CELLPHONE

电话 PHONE

邮箱 E-MAIL

地址 ADDRESS

名字 NAME

手机 CELLPHONE

电话 PHONE

邮箱 E-MAIL

地址 ADDRESS

名字 NAME

手机 CELLPHONE

电话 PHONE

邮箱 E-MAIL

地址 ADDRESS

名字 NAME

手机 CELLPHONE

电话 PHONE

邮箱 E-MAIL

地址 ADDRESS

名字 NAME

手机 CELLPHONE

电话 PHONE

邮箱 E-MAIL

地址 ADDRESS

名字 NAME

手机 CELLPHONE

电话 PHONE

邮箱 E-MAIL

地址 ADDRESS

名字 NAME

手机 CELLPHONE

电话 PHONE

邮箱 E-MAIL

地址 ADDRESS

名字 NAME

手机 CELLPHONE

电话 PHONE

邮箱 E-MAIL

地址 ADDRESS

名字 NAME

手机 CELLPHONE

电话 PHONE

邮箱 E-MAIL

地址 ADDRESS

名字 NAME

手机 CELLPHONE

电话 PHONE

邮箱 E-MAIL

地址 ADDRESS

名字 NAME

手机 CELLPHONE

电话 PHONE

邮箱 E-MAIL

地址 ADDRESS

名字 NAME

手机 CELLPHONE

电话 PHONE

邮箱 E-MAIL

地址 ADDRESS

名字 NAME

手机 CELLPHONE

电话 PHONE

邮箱 E-MAIL

地址 ADDRESS

名字 NAME

手机 CELLPHONE

电话 PHONE

邮箱 E-MAIL

地址 ADDRESS

名字 NAME

手机 CELLPHONE

电话 PHONE

邮箱 E-MAIL

地址 ADDRESS

名字 NAME

手机 CELLPHONE

电话 PHONE

邮箱 E-MAIL

地址 ADDRESS

名字 NAME

手机 CELLPHONE

电话 PHONE

邮箱 E-MAIL

地址 ADDRESS

名字 NAME

手机 CELLPHONE

电话 PHONE

邮箱 E-MAIL

地址 ADDRESS

名字 NAME

手机 CELLPHONE

电话 PHONE

邮箱 E-MAIL

地址 ADDRESS

名字 NAME

手机 CELLPHONE

电话 PHONE

邮箱 E-MAIL

地址 ADDRESS

名字 NAME

手机 CELLPHONE

电话 PHONE

邮箱 E-MAIL

地址 ADDRESS

名字 NAME

手机 CELLPHONE

电话 PHONE

邮箱 E-MAIL

地址 ADDRESS

名字 NAME

手机 CELLPHONE

电话 PHONE

邮箱 E-MAIL

地址 ADDRESS

名字 NAME

手机 CELLPHONE

电话 PHONE

邮箱 E-MAIL

地址 ADDRESS

名字 NAME

手机 CELLPHONE

电话 PHONE

邮箱 E-MAIL

地址 ADDRESS

名字 NAME

手机 CELLPHONE

电话 PHONE

邮箱 E-MAIL

地址 ADDRESS

名字 NAME

手机 CELLPHONE

电话 PHONE

邮箱 E-MAIL

地址 ADDRESS

名字 NAME

手机 CELLPHONE

电话 PHONE

邮箱 E-MAIL

地址 ADDRESS

名字 NAME

手机 CELLPHONE

电话 PHONE

邮箱 E-MAIL

地址 ADDRESS